This book belongs to...

Treasured Tales

p

CONTENTS

Little Red Riding Hood

Once upon a time there was a little girl who lived with her mother at the edge of a deep, dark forest. Everyone called the girl 'Little Red Riding Hood', because she always wore a bright red cloak with a bright red hood.

One sunny morning her mother said, "Granny isn't feeling very well. Please will you take this basket of goodies to her, to make her feel better?"

"I will," replied Little Red Riding Hood.

"Remember," said her mother, "stay on the path, and don't stop to talk to any strangers on the way."

Little Red Riding Hood hopped and skipped along the path to Granny's house. She had only gone a short way into the deep, dark forest, when a sly, nasty wolf with big shiny teeth and long sharp claws jumped out onto the path, right in front of her.

"Hello, my pretty one," said the wolf. "Where are you going on this fine morning?"

"Good morning," said Little Red Riding Hood politely. "I'm going to see my granny, who isn't feeling very well. She lives all the way on the other side of the forest. But please excuse me, I am not allowed to talk to strangers."

"Of course little girl," sneered the crafty wolf. "You must be in a hurry. Why not take a moment to pick a big bunch of these lovely wildflowers to cheer your granny up?"

"Thank you Mr Wolf, that sounds like a very good idea," said Little Red Riding Hood, putting her basket down on the ground. "I'm sure that Granny would love them."

So, while Little Red Riding Hood picked a bunch of sweet-smelling flowers, the wicked wolf raced ahead through the deep, dark forest and soon arrived at Granny's pretty cottage.

The wolf lifted the knocker and banged hard at the door.

Sweet old Granny sat up in bed. "Who is it?" she called.

"It's me, Little Red Riding Hood," replied the wolf in a voice just like Little Red Riding Hood's.

"Hello, my dear," called Granny. "The door is not locked—lift up the latch and come in."

So the wolf opened the door and, quick as a flash, he gobbled Granny up. Then he put on her nightie and nightcap, and crawled under the bedcovers to lie in wait for Little Red Riding Hood.

A short time later, Little Red Riding Hood arrived at the cottage and knocked on Granny's door.

"Who is it?" called the wolf, in a high voice just like Granny's.

"It's me, Granny," came the reply, "Little Red Riding Hood."

"Hello, my dear," called the wolf. "The door is not locked – lift up the latch and come in."

So Little Red Riding Hood lifted the latch, opened the door and went into Granny's cottage.

Little Red Riding Hood couldn't believe her eyes. "Oh, Granny," she said, "it is so nice to see you, but what big ears you have!"

"All the better to hear you with," said the wolf. "Come closer, my dear."

Little Red Riding Hood took a step closer to the bed.

"Oh, Granny," she said, "what big eyes you have!"

"All the better to see you with," said the wolf. "Come closer, my dear."

So Little Red Riding Hood took another step closer. Now she was right beside Granny's bed.

"Oh, Granny!" she cried. "What big teeth you have!

"All the better to eat you with, my dear!" snarled the wolf, and he jumped up and swallowed Little Red Riding Hood in one BIG gulp!

Now it just so happened that a woodcutter was passing Granny's cottage that sunny morning. He was going to work on the other side of the forest. He knew that Granny had not been feeling very well, so he decided to look in on her.

What a surprise he had when he saw the hairy wolf fast asleep in Granny's bed!

When he saw the wolf's big, fat tummy, he knew just what had happened.

Quick as a flash, he took out his shiny sharp axe and sliced the wolf open! Out popped Granny and Little Red Riding Hood, surprised and shaken, but safe and well.

The woodcutter dragged the wolf outside and threw him down a deep, dark well so he would never trouble anyone ever again. Then he, Granny and Little Red Riding Hood sat down to tea and ate all of the yummy goodies from Little Red Riding Hood's basket.

After tea, Little Red Riding Hood waved goodbye to her Granny and the woodcutter and ran all the way home to her mother, without straying once from the path or talking to any strangers. What an eventful day!

Jack and the Beanstalk

Jack was a lively young boy who lived with his mother in a tiny little cottage in the country.

Jack and his mother were very poor. They had straw on the floor, and many panes of glass in their windows were broken. The only thing of value that was left was a cow.

One day, Jack's mother called him in from the garden, where he was chopping logs for their stove. "You will have to take Daisy the cow to market and sell her," she said sadly.

As Jack trudged along the long road to market, he met a strange old man.

"Where are you taking that fine milking cow?" asked the man.

"To market, sir," replied Jack, "to sell her."

"If you sell her to me," said the man, "I will give you these beans. They are special, magic beans. You won't regret it, I promise."

When Jack heard the word "magic", he became very excited. He quickly swapped the cow for the beans, and ran all the way home.

Jack rushed through the cottage door. "Mother! Mother!" he called. "Where are you?"

"Why are you home so soon?" asked Jack's mother, coming down the stairs. "How much did you get for the cow?"

"I got these," said Jack, holding out his hand. "They're magic beans!"

"What?" shrieked his mother. "You sold our only cow for a handful of beans? You silly boy, come here!"

Angrily, she snatched the beans from Jack's hand and flung them out of the window and into the garden. Jack was sent to bed with no supper that night.

The next morning, Jack's rumbling stomach woke him early. His room was strangely dark. As he got dressed, he glanced out of his window — and what he saw took his breath away.

Overnight, a beanstalk had sprung up in the garden. Its trunk was almost as thick as Jack's cottage and its top was so tall that it disappeared into the clouds.

Jack yelled with excitement and rushed outside. As he began to climb the beanstalk, his mother stood at the bottom and begged for him to come back down.

At last, tired and very hungry, Jack reached the top. He found himself in a strange land full of clouds. He could see something glinting in the distance and began walking towards it.

He eventually came to the biggest castle he had ever seen. Maybe he could find some food in there?

He crept under the front door and ran straight into an enormous foot!

"What was that?" boomed a female voice, and the whole room shook. Jack found himself looking into a huge eye. Suddenly, he was whisked into the air by a giant hand!

"What are you?" roared the voice.

"I'm Jack," said Jack, "and I'm tired and hungry. Please can you give me something to eat and a place to rest for a while?"

The giant woman was a kind old lady and took pity on the tiny boy. "Don't make a sound," she whispered. "My husband doesn't like boys and will eat you if he finds you." Then she gave Jack a crumb of warm bread and a thimble full of hot soup.

He was just finishing the last drop when the woman said, "Quick! Hide in the cupboard! My husband's coming!"

From inside the dark cupboard, Jack could hear the approach of thundering footsteps. Then a deep voice bellowed, "Fee, fie, foe, fum, I smell the blood of an Englishman! Be he alive or be he dead, I'll grind his bones to make my bread!"

Jack peeped out through a knothole in the cupboard door, and saw a huge giant standing beside the table.

"Wife!" shouted the giant. "I can smell a boy in the house!"

"Nonsense, dear," said the giant's wife soothingly. "All you can smell is this lovely dinner I have made for you. Now sit down and eat."

When the giant had gobbled up his dinner and a huge bowl of pudding, he shouted, "Wife! Bring me my gold! I wish to count it!"

Jack saw the giant's wife bring out several enormous sacks of coins. The giant picked one up and tipped out a cascade of gold onto the table top.

Then Jack watched as the giant counted the coins, one by one. The giant began to stack them up in piles as he worked. After a while, he started to yawn, and not long after, Jack saw that he had fallen asleep. Soon he heard very loud snoring!

"It's time I made a move!" Jack said to himself. And, quick as a flash, he leapt out of the cupboard, grabbed a sack of gold, slid down the table leg and ran for the door.

But the giant's wife heard him. "Stop, thief!" she screamed at the top of her voice, which woke her husband. He jumped up in a hurry and ran after Jack, shouting loudly, "Come back!"

Jack ran until he came to the top of the beanstalk. Then, with the giant still after him, he scrambled down as fast as he could.

"Mother!" he called, as he got closer to the ground. "Mother, get the axe!"

By the time Jack reached the bottom, his mother was there with the axe. She quickly chopped down the beanstalk, and the giant came crashing down with it–he never got up again!

Now that they had the gold, Jack and his mother were very rich. They wouldn't have to worry about anything ever again and they lived happily ever after.

Sleeping Beauty

Once upon a time, in a land far, far away, there lived a king and queen who were kind and good. When the queen gave birth to a baby girl, the whole kingdom rejoiced.

When it was time for the baby to be christened, the king and queen arranged a great celebration. They asked the seven good fairies of the kingdom to be the baby's godmothers. But eight fairies arrived at the feast.

The eighth fairy was ugly and old, and no one had seen her for years. The king and queen, thinking she was dead, hadn't invited her to take part in the ceremony.

Soon it was time for the fairies to give the baby princess their magical presents. The first gave her the gift of beauty, the second gave her wisdom. The third fairy said she would be graceful, the fourth said that she would dance like the wind. The fifth and sixth gave her the gift of music and song, so that she would sing and play like an angel.

Just before the seventh fairy stepped up to give the princess her gift, the eighth fairy pushed ahead of her. " The princess," she cackled, "will prick her finger on the spindle of a spinning wheel – and die!"

Everyone in the room was horrified, and the queen began to cry. But then the seventh fairy stepped forward. "Here is my gift," she said. "The princess will not die. Instead, when she pricks her finger, she will fall asleep for a hundred years. At the end of that time, a prince will come to wake her up."

The king and queen were relieved, but even so they ordered every spinning wheel in the kingdom to be destroyed. They couldn't bear to think of anything hurting their daughter.

The years passed and the princess grew into a lovely young girl, as wise, beautiful and graceful as the fairies had promised.

On the day of her sixteenth birthday, she was wandering through the castle when she came to a small room in a tall tower. Inside, an old woman sat spinning thread.

"My dear," cackled the old woman, "come here and try this for yourself."

As soon as the princess's hand touched the spindle, she pricked her finger and fell to the floor in a deep sleep.

When they discovered their daughter, the king and queen were heartbroken, for they knew that she would not wake for a hundred years. They called for the palace guard, who gently laid the sleeping princess on a golden stretcher and carried her to the royal bedchamber. There they placed her on a bed with silken pillows and velvet covers. The king and queen watched over her and cried.

"Oh, my dear," said the queen to her husband. "How are we ever going to cope without our darling daughter?"

The fairy who had saved the princess's life heard what had happened. Worried that the princess would wake up in a world where she knew no one, she cast a spell over the whole castle. Everyone, from the guards and the kitchen maids to the gardeners and the cooks—even the princess's pet dog—fell into a deep, deep sleep.

Then the fairy made tall trees and twisting, sharp brambles grow around the castle, surrounding it with a thick thorny wall that no one could get through. Only the very tops of the castle's towers could be seen.

And so a hundred years went by.

One day, a prince from a nearby land was out riding when he saw the tops of the castle towers rising from the middle of the thick, dark wood. He asked some of the country people about it, and they told him the story of the Sleeping Beauty.

"Many people have wanted to get through those thorns," they told him, "but they have all died trying."

The prince was determined to be the one who succeeded and set off towards the mysterious castle.

To the prince's amazement, the thorny brambles and the twisting branches of the dark trees let him pass through easily. He reached the castle door, and went inside.

The prince walked through many halls and chambers where people and animals slept as if they were dead. He searched every room and chamber, until he found the very one where the beautiful princess slept.

"Oh, princess!" cried the prince. "You are more beautiful than the most delicate rose ever found."

The prince moved quietly towards the sleeping princess and gazed down lovingly at her. He gently took her tiny hand in his, and as love filled his heart, he knelt beside her and slowly kissed her red lips. Instantly the princess's eyes opened.

"Is it you, my prince?" she said, when she saw him. "I have waited such a long time for you!"

At that moment the spell was broken, and everyone else in the castle woke up, too.

That evening, the princess's sixteenth birthday was celebrated with a joyous party – just a hundred years too late!

The princess and her prince danced together all evening, and soon after, were married. They lived together in happiness for many, many years.

The Three Little Pigs

Once upon a time, there were three little pigs who lived with their mummy in a big stone house.

One day, Mummy Pig said, "Children, it's time for you to go out and find your fortune in the big wide world." So she packed a little bag of food and a drink for each of them, and sent them on their way.

"Goodbye!" she called, as the three little pigs set off on their adventure. "Good luck, my dears, and remember to watch out for the big, bad wolf!"

"We will, Mummy," called the little pigs as they waved goodbye.

After a while, the three little pigs stopped for a rest and decided that they should each build a house to live in. Just then, they saw a farmer coming along the road with a wagon full of golden straw.

"Please, sir," said the first little pig, "may I have some of your straw to build myself a house?"

"Yes, little pig," said the farmer, "of course you can."

So the first little pig built his house of straw. Soon it was finished. It looked very good indeed, and the first little pig was happy.

The other two little pigs set off on their journey together and, after a while, they met a man carrying a large bundle of sticks.

"Please, sir," said the second little pig, "may I have some of your sticks to build myself a house?"

"Yes, little pig," said the man, "of course you can."

So the second little pig built his house of sticks. Soon it was finished. It looked very good indeed, and the second little pig was happy.

The third little pig set off on his journey alone. He saw lots of people with wagons of straw and bundles of sticks, but he did not stop until he met a man with a cart filled to the brim with bricks.

"Please, sir," said the third little pig, "may I have some bricks to build myself a house?"

"Yes, little pig," said the man, "of course you can."

So the third little pig built his house of bricks. Soon it was finished. It looked very good indeed. It was strong and solid, and the third little pig was very, very pleased.

That evening, the big, bad wolf was walking along the road. He was very hungry and looking for something good to eat. He saw the first little pig's house of straw and looked in through the window.

"Yum, yum," he said to himself, licking his lips. "This little pig would make a most tasty dinner."

So in his friendliest voice, the wolf called through the window, "Little pig, little pig, please let me in!"

But the first little pig remembered his Mummy's warning, so he replied, "No, no, I won't let you in, not by the hair on my chinny-chin-chin!"

This made the wolf really angry. "Very well!" he roared. "I'll huff and I'll puff, and I'll blow your house down!"

The poor little pig was very afraid, but he still would not let the wolf in. So the wolf huffed… and he puffed… and he BLEW the straw house down.

Then the big, bad wolf chased the little pig and – gobbled him up!

But the wolf was still hungry! He walked down the road and soon came to the house made of sticks. He looked through the window and called to the second little pig, "Little pig, little pig, please let me in."

"No, no!" cried the second little pig. "I won't let you in, not by the hair on my chinny-chin-chin!"

"Very well," cried the wolf. "Then I'll huff and I'll puff, and I'll blow your house down!"

And that's just what the big, bad wolf did. He huffed… and he puffed… and he BLEW the stick house down! Then he gobbled up the second little pig.

But the big, bad wolf was still hungry. So he walked down the road and soon came to the house made of bricks. He looked through the window and called to the third little pig, "Little pig, little pig, please let me in."

"No, no!" cried the third little pig. "I won't let you in, not by the hair on my chinny-chin-chin!"

"Very well," roared the big, bad wolf. "I'll huff and I'll puff, and I'll blow your house down!"

So the wolf huffed and he puffed... he HUFFED and he PUFFED... and he HUFFED and he PUFFED some more, but he could not blow the brick house down!

By now the big, bad wolf was very, very angry. He scrambled up onto the roof and began to climb down through the chimney.

But the third little pig was a clever little pig, and he had put a big pot of boiling water to bubble on the fire.

When the wolf came down the chimney, he landed – ker-splosh! – right in the middle of the pot of boiling water! He burned his bottom so badly that he ran out of the house and down the road as fast as his legs could carry him, and was never heard of again!

The third little pig was very pleased
with his house of bricks and lived in it
for many years, happy and content.
And nothing was heard of the big,
bad wolf ever again.

Snow White

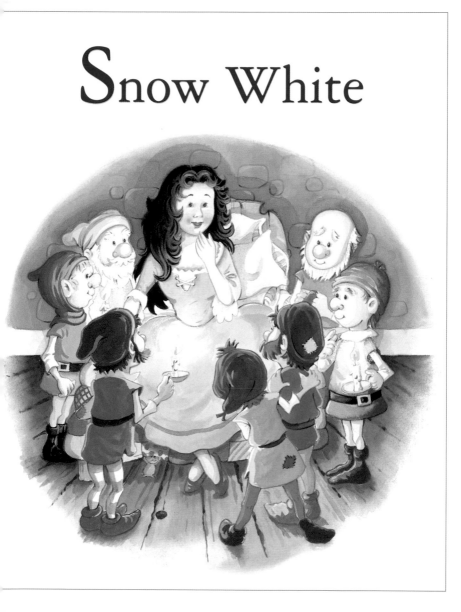

Long, long ago, in a faraway land, there lived a king and queen who had a beautiful baby girl. Her lips were as red as cherries, her hair as black as coal and her skin as white as snow – her name was Snow White.

Sadly, the queen died and years later the king married again. The new queen was very beautiful, but also evil, cruel and vain. She had a magic mirror, and every day she looked into it and asked, "Mirror, mirror on the wall, who is the fairest one of all?"

And every day, the mirror replied, "You, O Queen, are the fairest!"

Time passed, and every year Snow White grew more beautiful by the hour. The queen became increasingly jealous of her stepdaughter.

One day, the magic mirror gave the queen a different answer to her question. "Snow White is the fairest one of all!" it replied.

The queen was furious. She ordered her huntsman to take Snow White deep into the forest and kill her.

But the huntsman couldn't bear to harm Snow White. "Run away!" he told her. "Run away and never come back, or the queen will kill us both!" Snow White fled deep into the forest.

As Snow White rushed through the trees she came upon a tiny cottage. She knocked at the door and then went in – the house was empty. There she found a tiny table with seven tiny chairs. Upstairs there were seven little beds. Exhausted, she lay down across them and fell asleep.

Many hours later, Snow White woke to see seven little faces peering at her. The dwarfs, who worked in a diamond mine, had returned home and wanted to know who the pretty young girl was.

Snow White told them her story and why she had to run away. They all sat round and listened to her tale.

When she had finished, the eldest dwarf said, "If you will look after our house for us, we will keep you safe. But please don't let anyone into the cottage while we are at work!"

The next morning, when the wicked queen asked the mirror her usual question, she was horrified when it answered, "The fairest is Snow White, gentle and good. She lives in a cottage, deep in the wood!"

The queen turned green with rage; she had been tricked. She magically disguised herself as an old pedlar and set off into the wood to seek out Snow White and kill the girl herself.

That afternoon, Snow White heard a tap-tapping at the window. She looked out and saw an old woman with a basket full of bright ribbons and laces.

"Pretty things for sale," cackled the old woman.

Snow White remembered the dwarfs' warning. But the ribbons and laces were so lovely, and the woman seemed so harmless, that she let her in.

"Try this new lace in your dress, my dear," said the old woman. Snow White was thrilled and let the lady thread the laces. But they were pulled so tight that Snow White fainted.

Certain that at last she had killed her stepdaughter, the queen raced through the forest, back to her castle, laughing evilly.

That evening, the dwarfs returned home. They were shocked to discover Snow White lying on the floor – lifeless. They loosened the laces on her dress so she could breathe and made her promise once again not to let any strangers in when they were at work.

The next day, when the mirror told the queen that Snow White was still alive, she was livid and vowed to kill her once and for all. She disguised herself and went back to the cottage.

This time the old woman took with her a basket of lovely red apples. She had poisoned the biggest, reddest one of all. She knocked on the door and called out, "Juicy red apples for sale."

The apples looked so delicious that Snow White just had to buy one. She opened the door and let the old woman in. "My, what pretty, rosy cheeks you have, deary," said the woman, "the very colour of my apples. Here, take a bite and see how good they are." She handed Snow White the biggest one...

Snow White took a large bite and fell to the floor – dead. The old woman fled into the forest, happy at last.

This time, the dwarfs could not bring Snow White back to life. Overcome with grief, they placed her gently in a glass coffin and carried it to a quiet clearing in the forest. And there they sat, keeping watch over their beloved Snow White.

One day, a handsome young prince came riding through the forest and saw the beautiful young girl in the glass coffin. He fell in love with her at once and begged the dwarfs to let him take her back to his castle.

At first the dwarfs refused, but when they saw how much the prince loved their Snow White, they agreed.

As the prince lifted the coffin to carry it away, he stumbled, and the piece of poisoned apple fell from Snow White's mouth, where it had been lodged all this time. Snow White's eyes fluttered open, and she looked up and saw the handsome young man.

"Where am I?" she asked him in a bewildered voice. "Who are you?"

"I am your prince," he said. "And you are safe with me now. Please will you marry me and come to live in my castle!" He leant forward and kissed her cheek.

"Oh, yes sweet prince," cried Snow White. "Of course I will."

The next day, the magic mirror told the wicked queen of Snow White's good fortune. She flew into a rage and disappeared in a flash of lightning.

Snow White married her prince, and went to live in his castle. The seven dwarfs visited them often, and Snow White and her prince lived happily ever after.

Rumpelstiltskin

Once upon a time there was a boastful miller. One day, he told the king that his daughter was so clever that she could spin gold out of straw.

"I must meet this remarkable girl," said the king. "Bring her to the palace at once."

The king took the miller's daughter to a room filled with straw. In one corner stood a spinning wheel. "You must spin all this straw into gold before morning," the king told the girl, "or you will be put to death." Then he went out and locked the door behind him.

The poor girl sat at the spinning wheel and wept. However could she make gold from straw? Suddenly, the door flew open, and in leapt a funny-looking little man.

"Why are you crying?" he asked.

When the girl had told him what the king had said, the strange man replied, "What will you give me if I spin this straw into gold for you?"

"My pearl necklace," said the girl.

So the little man sat down at the spinning wheel and quickly spun all the straw into gold. Then he magically vanished from the room.

The next morning, the king was amazed at all the gold – but now he wanted even more. So he took the girl to a bigger room, and had it filled with straw. Once again, he told her to spin the straw into gold by morning, or she would die. Then he left.

The poor girl sat down and wept. Suddenly, the odd little man appeared, "What will you give me if I help you this time?" he asked.

"My pretty ring," the girl replied.

So the little man began to spin, and soon all the straw had turned into gold. Then he vanished.

The next morning the greedy king was astounded but still not satisfied. So he took the girl to an even bigger room, piled to the ceiling with straw. "If you succeed this time, you will become queen," the king said. "If you fail, you know what will happen."

As soon as the girl was alone, the little man appeared. "I have nothing left to give you," said the girl.

"Then promise me your first-born child when you become queen," said the man.

"I might never become queen and I may never have a child," the girl thought, and so she promised.

So the strange little man sat down at the spinning wheel and began to work. He spun for many hours and the pile of gold grew and grew.

"At last," said the little man, "my task is done." Then he vanished. The girl gazed around the room. It was stacked from floor to ceiling with glistening gold that shone like the sun.

At dawn, the king was overjoyed. He kept his promise and soon married the miller's daughter.

The whole kingdom rejoiced, and the king and his new queen were very happy together.

A year later, the king and queen had a baby. By this time, the queen had forgotten all about her promise — but the funny little man had not. One night, he appeared in the queen's bedchamber. "I have come for your baby!" he announced gleefully.

"No!" cried the queen. "I will give you jewels, gold, anything you wish! But please do not take my baby." She wept so miserably that the little man took pity on her.

"Very well," he said. "If you can guess my name within three nights you may keep your baby. If not, the child is mine!" Then he disappeared.

The queen sent messengers out to gather names from every town and village in the kingdom. They returned with thousands of suggestions. Over the next two evenings, when the little man arrived, the queen questioned him again and again;

"Is your name Tom?"

"No," replied the little man.

"Jack? Dick? Peter?" she asked. The strange man shook his head. "Could it be Brutus or Clarence, then?"

Each time, the reply was the same: "No, Your Majesty."

By the third day, only one messenger had not returned. Late that afternoon, he was on his way back to the palace when he saw a hut in a forest clearing. In front of it, an odd little man was dancing around a fire, singing:

"I'll be the winner of this game!
The queen will never guess my name!
She will lose, and I will win,
Because my name is...
Rumpelstiltskin!"

The messenger galloped back to the palace and told the queen what he had seen and heard. She was so grateful that she rewarded the messenger with a huge sack of gold.

That night, the queen eagerly waited in her throne room for the little man. When he appeared, the queen asked, "Is your name Guzzletum?"

"No, it's not!" laughed the little man.

"Is it Bumblebottom? Jigglejoggle? Tickletooth or Wigglewoggle?"

"No! No!" he cackled. "Your time's running out, Your Majesty!"

The queen smiled. "Could it be... Rumpelstiltskin?"

The little man could not believe his ears and flew into a rage. "Who told you? Who told you?" he shrieked. "How did you find out?"

He cried and squealed and beat the floor with his fists.

"You've won! You've won!" he wailed, and disappeared in a shower of sparks.

The little man never came back to worry the queen again, and they all lived happily ever after.

Cinderella

Once upon a time, there lived a pretty little girl. When she was young, her mother sadly died. Her father remarried, but the girl's stepmother was a mean woman with two ugly daughters. These stepsisters were so jealous of the young girl's beauty that they treated her like a servant and made her sit among the cinders in the kitchen.

They called her Cinderella, and before long everyone, even her father, had forgotten the little girl's real name. Cinderella missed her real mother more and more each day.

127

One day, an invitation arrived from the royal palace. The king and queen were holding a ball for the prince's twenty-first birthday, and all the fine ladies of the kingdom were invited.

Cinderella's stepsisters were very excited when their invitations arrived.

"I will wear my red velvet gown!" cried the first stepsister. "And the black pearl necklace that Mother gave to me."

"And I will wear my blue silk dress!" cried the other. "With a silver tiara."

"Come, Cinderella!" they called. "You must help us to get ready!"

Cinderella helped her stepsisters with their silk stockings and frilly petticoats. She brushed and curled their hair and powdered their cheeks and noses. At last, she squeezed them into their beautiful ball-gowns.

But even after all this, the two ugly stepsisters weren't nearly as lovely as Cinderella was in her rags. This made them very jealous and angry, and they began to tease Cinderella.

"Too bad you can't come to the ball, Cinders!" sneered the first stepsister.

"Yes," laughed the other one. "They'd never let a shabby creature like you near the palace!"

Cinderella said nothing, but inside, her heart was breaking. She really wanted to go to the ball. After her stepsisters left, she sat and wept.

"Dry your tears, my dear," said a gentle voice.

Cinderella was amazed. A kind old woman stood before her. In her hand was a sparkly wand that shone.

"I am your Fairy Godmother," she told Cinderella. "And you shall go to the ball!"

"But I have nothing to wear! And how will I get there?" cried Cinderella.

The Fairy Godmother smiled!

The Fairy Godmother asked Cinders to fetch her the biggest pumpkin in the garden. With a flick of her magic wand she turned it into a golden carriage and the mice in the kitchen mousetrap into fine horses. A fat rat soon became a handsome coachman.

Cinderella couldn't believe her eyes.

Smiling, the Fairy Godmother waved her wand once more and suddenly Cinderella was dressed in a splendid ball-gown. On her feet were sparkling glass slippers.

"My magic will end at midnight, so you must be home before then," said the Fairy Godmother. "Good luck."

When Cinderella arrived at the ball, everyone was dazzled by her beauty. Whispers went round the ballroom as the other guests wondered who this enchanting stranger could be. Even Cinderella's own stepsisters did not recognise her.

As soon as the prince set eyes on Cinderella, he fell in love with her. "Would you do me the honour of this dance?" he asked.

"Why certainly, sir," Cinderella answered. And from that moment on he only had eyes for Cinderella.

Soon the clock struck midnight.
"I must go!" said Cinderella, suddenly
remembering her promise to her
Fairy Godmother. She fled from the
ballroom and ran down the palace
steps. The prince ran after her, but
when he got outside, she was gone.
He didn't notice a grubby servant
girl holding a pumpkin. A few mice
and a rat scurried around her feet.

But there on the steps was one dainty
glass slipper. The prince picked it up
and rushed back into the palace.
"Does anyone know who this slipper
belongs to?" he cried.

The next day, Cinderella's stepsisters could talk of nothing but the ball, and the beautiful stranger who had danced all night with the prince. As they were talking, there was a knock at the door.

"Cinderella," called the stepmother, "quick, jump to it and see who it is." Standing on the doorstep was His Highness the Prince and a royal footman, who was holding the little glass slipper on a velvet cushion.

"The lady whose foot this slipper fits is my one and only true love," said the prince. "I am visiting every house in the kingdom in search of her."

The two stepsisters began shoving each other out of the way in their rush to try on the slipper. They both squeezed and pushed as hard as they could, but their clumsy feet were far too big for the tiny glass shoe.

Then Cinderella stepped forward. "Please, Your Highness," she said, shyly, "may I try?"

As her stepsisters watched in utter amazement, Cinderella slid her foot into the dainty slipper. It fitted as if it were made for her!

As the prince gazed into her eyes, he knew he had found his love – and Cinderella knew she had found hers.

Cinderella and the prince soon set a date to be married.

On the day of their wedding, the land rang to the sound of bells, and the sun shone as the people cheered. Even Cinderella's nasty stepsisters were invited. Everyone had a really wonderful day, and Cinderella and her prince lived happily ever after.

Puss in Boots

There was once a miller who had three sons. When he died, he left his mill to the eldest son, his cottage to his middle son and only his pet cat to his youngest son, William.

William went and sat under a tree, feeling very miserable and sorry for himself. "What will become of us, Puss?" he moaned.

To William's utter amazement, Puss answered him. "Don't worry, Master," said the cat. "Just do what I say and you will be far richer than either of your brothers!"

Puss told William to get him a fine suit of clothes, a pair of soft leather boots and a strong canvas sack. Then he caught a huge rabbit, put it in the sack, and took it to the palace.

No one there had ever seen a talking cat before, so he was granted an immediate audience with the king.

"Your Majesty," said Puss, "this fine rabbit is a gift from my master, the Marquis of Carabas."

The king had never heard of the Marquis of Carabas, but he was too embarrassed to admit this. "Please thank the Marquis," he said to Puss, "and give him my regards."

The next day, Puss caught some plump partridges and once more he took them to the king, with the same message: "These are from my master."

For several months, Puss went on bringing the king fine gifts.

One day, he heard that the king would be riding along the river bank that afternoon with the princess.

"Master," said Puss, "you must go swimming in the river today."

"Why?" asked William.

"Just do as I say, and you will see," answered Puss.

While William was swimming, Puss hid all his clothes. Then, when he saw the king's carriage approaching, he ran up to it shouting for help. "Help!" cried Puss. "Robbers have stolen my master's clothes!"

When the king recognised the cat, he immediately called to his chief steward and ordered him to bring a fine new suit from the palace.

"It must be of the finest cut," said the king, "and made from the softest cloth, do you hear! Only the best will do for the Marquis of Carabas!"

Once he was dressed in his fine new suit, William looked quite handsome. The princess invited him to join her and her father in the carriage.

As William and the princess sat side by side, they began to fall in love.

Meanwhile, Puss ran ahead until he came to a meadow where he saw some men mowing. "The king's carriage is coming," Puss told them. "When he asks whose meadow this is, say it belongs to the Marquis of Carabas — or you will have your heads cut off!"

The mowers didn't dare to disobey.

When the royal carriage came by, the king asked who the meadow belonged to. The mowers quickly replied, "The Marquis of Carabas."

"I can see that you are very well off indeed," the king said to William, who blushed modestly. That made the princess love him even more!

Down the road, Puss came to a field where men were harvesting corn.

"When the king asks whose corn this is," Puss told them, "say it belongs to the Marquis of Carabas – or you will have your heads cut off!"

The harvesters didn't dare to disobey.

Next, Puss came to an enormous castle which he knew belonged to a fierce ogre. Still he bravely knocked on the door.

When the ogre let him in, Puss bowed low and said, "I have heard that you have wondrous powers, and can change yourself into anything — even a lion or an elephant."

"That is true," said the ogre. And to prove it, he changed himself into a snarling, growling lion.

Puss was terrified and leapt up onto a cupboard. Then the ogre changed himself back again.

"That was amazing," Puss remarked. "But surely it cannot be too difficult for someone of your size to change into a creature as big as a lion. If you were truly the magician they say you are, you could turn into something tiny – like a mouse."

"Of course I can do that!" bellowed the ogre. In an instant he became a little brown mouse scurrying across the floor.

Quick as a flash, Puss leapt off the cupboard, pounced on the mouse and ate it in one big gulp!

Soon, Puss heard the king's carriage drawing near and rushed outside. As it approached, he bowed low and said, "Welcome, Your Majesty, to the home of the Marquis of Carabas."

The king was very impressed indeed. "May we come in?" he asked William.

"Of course, Your Majesty," replied William, a little confused.

As they walked through the castle, the King was delighted to see treasures of great value everywhere he looked. He was so pleased that he said to William, "You are the perfect husband for my daughter."

William and the princess were very happy and later that day they were married. They lived in the ogre's castle happily ever after. Puss, of course, lived with them – though he never chased mice again!

Goldilocks and the Three Bears

Once upon a time, deep in a dark green forest, there lived a family of bears. There was great big Daddy Bear. There was middle-sized Mummy Bear. And there was little Baby Bear.

One sunny morning, the bears were up early, hungry for their breakfast. Daddy Bear cooked three bowls of porridge. He made it with lots of golden, runny honey, just the way bears like it. "Breakfast is ready!" called Daddy Bear.

But when he poured it into the bowls, it was far too hot to eat!

"We'll just have to let our porridge
cool down for a while before we eat
it," said Mummy Bear.

"But I'm hungry!" wailed Baby Bear.

"I know, let's go for a walk in the
forest while we wait," suggested
Mummy Bear. "Get the basket, Baby
Bear. We can gather some wild berries
as we go."

So, leaving the steaming bowls of
porridge on the table, the three bears
went out into the forest. The last one
out was little Baby Bear, and he forgot
to close the front door behind him.

The sun was shining brightly through the trees that morning and someone else was walking in the forest. It was a little girl called Goldilocks, who had long, curly golden hair and the cutest nose you ever did see.

Goldilocks was skipping happily through the forest when suddenly she smelt something yummy and delicious – whatever could it be?

She followed the smell until she came to the three bears' cottage. It seemed to be coming from inside. The door was open, so she peeped in and saw three bowls of porridge on the table.

Goldilocks just couldn't resist the lovely sweet smell. So, even though she knew she wasn't ever supposed to go into anyone's house without first being invited, she tiptoed inside.

First, she tasted the porridge in Daddy Bear's great big bowl. "Ouch!" she said. "This porridge is *far* too hot!" So she tried the porridge in Mummy Bear's middle-sized bowl. "Yuck!" said Goldilocks. "This porridge is *far* too sweet!" Finally, she tried the porridge in Baby Bear's tiny little bowl. "Yummy!" she said, licking her lips. "This porridge is *just right*!" So Goldilocks ate it *all* up – every last drop!

Goldilocks was so full up after eating Baby Bear's porridge that she decided she must sit down. First, she tried sitting in Daddy Bear's great big chair. "Oh, dear!" she said. "This chair is *far* too hard!" So she tried Mummy Bear's middle-sized chair. "Oh, no!" said Goldilocks. "This chair is *far* too soft!" Finally, Goldilocks tried Baby Bear's tiny little chair. "Hurray!" she cried. "This chair is *just right*!" So she stretched out and made herself very comfortable.

But Baby Bear's chair wasn't *just right*! It was *far* too small and, as Goldilocks settled down, it broke into lots of little pieces!

Goldilocks picked herself up off the floor and brushed down her dress. Trying out all of those chairs had made her *very* tired. She looked around the cottage for a place to lie down and soon found the three bears' bedroom.

First, Goldilocks tried Daddy Bear's great big bed. "Oh, this won't do!" she said. "This bed is *far* too hard!" So she tried Mummy Bear's middle-sized bed. "Oh, bother!" said Goldilocks. "This bed is *far* too soft!" Finally, she tried Baby Bear's tiny little bed. "Yippee!" she cried. "This bed is *just right*!" So Goldilocks climbed in, pulled the blanket up to her chin and fell fast, fast asleep.

Not long after, the three bears came home from their walk, ready for their yummy porridge. But as soon as they entered their little cottage, they knew something wasn't quite right.

"Someone's been eating my porridge!" said Daddy Bear, when he looked at his great big bowl.

"Someone's been eating my porridge!" said Mummy Bear, looking at her middle-sized bowl.

"Someone's been eating *my* porridge," cried Baby Bear, looking sadly at his tiny little bowl. "And they've eaten it *all up*!"

Then Daddy Bear noticed that his chair had been moved. "Look, Mummy Bear! Someone's been sitting in my chair!" he said in his deep, gruff voice.

"Look, Daddy Bear! Someone's been sitting in my chair," said Mummy Bear, as she straightened the cushions on it.

"Someone's been sitting in *my* chair, too," cried Baby Bear. "And look! They've broken it all to pieces!" They all stared at the bits of broken chair. Then Baby Bear burst into tears.

Suddenly, the three bears heard the tiniest of noises. Was it a creak? Was it a groan? No, it was a snore, and it was coming from their bedroom. They crept up the stairs very, very quietly, to see what was making the noise…

"Someone's been sleeping in my bed!" cried Daddy Bear.

"Someone's been sleeping in my bed," said Mummy Bear.

"Someone's been sleeping in *my* bed!" cried Baby Bear. "And she's still there!"

All this noise woke Goldilocks up with a start.

When she saw the three bears standing over her, Goldilocks was very scared. "Oh, dear! Oh, dear! Oh, dear!" she cried, jumping out of Baby Bear's bed. She ran out of the bedroom, down the stairs, out of the front door and all the way back home – and she never ever came back to the forest again!

The
Elves and the
Shoemaker

Once upon a time there was a kind old shoemaker who lived in a tiny flat above his shop with his wife. He had many bills to pay, so he had to work from dawn to dusk to pay them off. The day came when he had only a few pennies left – just enough to buy leather for one final pair of shoes.

That evening, by candlelight, the shoemaker cut up the leather. Then, leaving it on his workbench, he picked up his candle and wearily climbed the stairs to his bed.

187

The next morning, when he came down to his shop, the shoemaker could not believe his eyes. There on his workbench, where the leather had been, was the finest pair of shoes he had ever seen.

The shoemaker went to the stairs and called to his wife to come and see what he had found. "Did you make these shoes?" he asked her.

"Of course not," she replied.

The shoemaker was very puzzled and scratched his head in amazement. "Then who could it have been?" he wondered.

The shoemaker put the shoes in his shop window. That afternoon, a fine gentleman came to try them on. He liked the shoes very much, and gave the shoemaker a good price for them.

With the money, the shoemaker was able to buy food for dinner, and had enough left over to buy leather to make two new pairs of shoes.

Later that night, the shoemaker cut up the leather and left it lying on his workbench. "I'll finish the shoes in the morning," he yawned, shutting up the shop. He picked up the candle and went up the stairs to bed.

The next morning, when he came downstairs, the shoemaker was truly amazed. There, sitting neatly on his workbench, were two fine pairs of beautiful new shoes! They were soft and delicate. He thought they were the best shoes he had ever seen.

Once again, the shoemaker called his wife and asked if she had made them. "Oh husband," she said, "of course I didn't."

The shoemaker was confused, but once again he put them in his shop window, where everyone could see them. In no time at all, he had sold both pairs for a very good price.

That evening, the shoemaker and his wife had a marvellous dinner. There was also enough money left to buy leather to make four new pairs of shoes!

Once more, the shoemaker cut out the leather and left it neatly on his workbench. And in the morning, there were more new shoes waiting for him when he came downstairs.

So it went on for weeks. Every night the shoemaker cut out the leather and left it on his workbench, and every morning there were splendid shoes waiting to be sold.

Soon the shoemaker and his wife were quite wealthy. But they still did not know who was making the smart shoes that appeared in the shop as if by magic.

One cold, wintry night, just before Christmas, the shoemaker and his wife decided that they had to solve the mystery once and for all. So, after the shoemaker left the leather on his workbench, he shut up the shop and hid in a big cupboard with his wife. They left the door slightly open so that they could see, and waited… and waited… and waited.

When the clock struck midnight, there was a tiny noise from the dark chimney. It grew louder. Suddenly, two tiny elves appeared in a shower of magical stars. They ran straight to the workbench and began to stitch and sew, until they had made five beautiful pairs of shoes.

They sang as they worked:
"There isn't any time to lose,
We must make these fine new shoes!"

As soon as the shoes were finished, they hopped off the workbench and shot up the chimney. The shoemaker and his wife were amazed.

The shoemaker and his wife wanted to do something in return for the kind little elves. What could they do?

"They must be frozen in those thin, tattered clothes," said the shoemaker.

"Yes," said his wife. "And their feet are bare, although they make shoes!"

So the shoemaker's wife made two little jackets and two pairs of trousers. She knitted four little woolly socks to keep their feet warm, and two tiny hats for their heads. The shoemaker made two pairs of small boots, fastened with shiny silver buckles.

That evening, they wrapped the little clothes in tissue paper and left them on the workbench. Then they hid in the cupboard and waited.

At the stroke of midnight, the elves appeared. They were puzzled when they saw parcels instead of leather. But when they opened the presents, they were overjoyed. They put on their new clothes and danced around the shop, singing,

"See what handsome boys we are!
We will work on shoes no more!"

They danced happily across the room, flew up the chimney and were gone in a flash!

The elves did not return, but the man and his wife never forgot the two tiny men and all their hard work.

The shoemaker continued to make shoes which were fine and beautiful, and he became rich and famous across the land. But none compared to the light and delicate shoes that the little elves had made!

Beauty
and the Beast

Once upon a time there was a man who lived in a cottage in the country with his three daughters. His youngest daughter was so pretty that everyone called her "Beauty", which made her two sisters very angry and jealous.

One day the man had to go to the city. Before he left, he told his daughters that he would bring each of them back a present and asked what they would like.

"Jewels!" the eldest daughter demanded. "Silk dresses!" said the second daughter. But all Beauty asked for was a single white rose.

On his return home, the father was caught in a snowstorm and lost his way. The blizzard was so thick and fierce and the forest so large and dark that he nearly gave up hope of ever finding his home. Then, through the mist, he glimpsed a grand palace.

He staggered to the great door – there seemed to be no one about. Inside, he found a table laid with a magnificent dinner. The man ate hungrily, then searched the house. Upstairs, he found a huge bed where he gratefully fell into an exhausted sleep. In the morning, when he awoke, breakfast was waiting beside the bed.

As he set off on his way home he noticed a wonderful rose garden. Remembering Beauty's request, he stopped to pick a white rose. Suddenly, with a mighty roar, a terrifying, snarling Beast appeared.

"I have welcomed you with every comfort," he growled, "and in return you steal my roses!"

Shaking with fear, the man begged for forgiveness. "I only wanted the rose as a present for my daughter!"

"I will spare you," said the Beast, "but only if your daughter comes to live here of her own free will. If not, you must return in three months."

Back home, the man tearfully told his daughters what had happened. To his surprise, Beauty agreed to go.

When she arrived at the palace, a glorious meal was waiting for her. "The Beast must want to fatten me," she thought. But she sat and ate.

As soon as Beauty finished her meal, the Beast appeared. He was truly horrifying, and she was frightened.

"Your room is all ready," said the Beast, and he led her to a door that said "Beauty's Room" in gold letters.

The room was everything Beauty could have wished for. She saw a little piano, beautiful silk dresses and fresh, fragrant roses. On the dressing table was a mirror with these words on it:

If anything you long to see,
Speak your wish, and look in me.

"I wish I could see my father," said Beauty, and instantly saw her father in the mirror, sitting sadly beside the fire at home.

"Perhaps the Beast doesn't mean to kill me after all," Beauty thought. "I wonder what he does want?"

The next evening the Beast joined Beauty for supper. "Tell me," he said, "am I truly horrible to look at?"

Beauty could not lie. "You are," she said. "But I know you are very kind-hearted."

"Then," said the Beast, "will you marry me?"

Beauty was surprised. She knew he might be angry if she refused, but she couldn't say yes as she didn't love him. "No," she said, "I will not marry you."

The Beast sighed so heavily that the walls shook. "Good night, then," he said sadly. And he left her to finish her dinner alone.

Beauty was very happy living in the palace. But one day, Beauty saw in her magic mirror that her father was ill. She begged the Beast to let her go home, and sadly he agreed.

"Take this magic ring," he told her. "If you want to come back, put it by your bedside and when you wake up, you will be here."

"I will come back," she promised.

Beauty looked after her father, and soon he was better. But one night, Beauty dreamt that the Beast was lying dead in his garden. Beauty woke up in tears and knew then that she loved the Beast.

Putting the magic ring by her bedside, Beauty closed her eyes.

When she opened them again, Beauty was in the Beast's garden – and he was lying on the ground.

"Oh, Beast," she cried, taking him in her arms, "please don't die! I love you, and I want to marry you!"

All at once light and music filled the air, and the Beast vanished. In his place stood a handsome prince.

"Who are you?" cried Beauty.

"I was your Beast," said the prince. "An evil witch cast a spell on me and turned me into that poor animal. The spell could only be broken when a beautiful girl agreed to marry me."

A few days later they were married, and Beauty's family came to join in the joyous celebrations at the palace.

Beauty had never been so happy. She loved the prince with all her heart, and they lived in their rose palace happily ever after.

This is a Parragon Book
This edition published in 2004

Parragon
Queen Street House
4 Queen Street
Bath, BA1 1HE, UK

Created by The Complete Works
Written by Aneurin Rhys and Ronne Randall
Illustrated by Chameleon Design

ISBN 1-40542-646-2
Printed in China